THE DONKEY'S GONE!
based on a story by
RUMI

text
OMid AraBian

illustrations
SHiLLa SHaKOORi

new york • oakland • london

Once upon a time, there was a man named Saleem the Sufi. (A Sufi is someone who spends their life looking for truth and the meaning of everything, instead of trying to own more and more things.)

Saleem the Sufi
had nothing in this world,
except a donkey that he
loved very much.

He traveled around on his donkey,
looking to learn everything he could about life.

Late one afternoon, cold and tired
from the day's journey, Saleem arrived
at a *khaneqah*—a place where Sufis gather
and sometimes stay for the night.
He decided to rest there until morning.

Saleem left his donkey with the stable boy.
"Please take good care of my donkey," he said.
"She's all I have in this world."
"I will," said the stable boy.

Then he entered
the *khaneqah*,
and was happy to see that
there were many other Sufis
staying there as well.

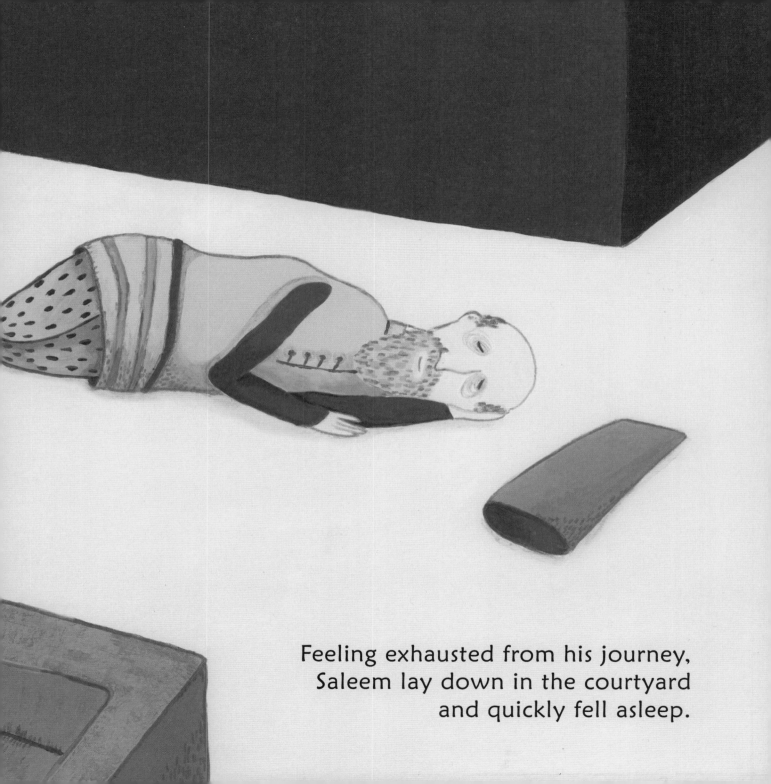

Feeling exhausted from his journey,
Saleem lay down in the courtyard
and quickly fell asleep.

When he woke up from his nap,
Saleem was surprised to see
that a big celebration had started.
There were tables full of food,
and a band of musicians
was getting ready to play.

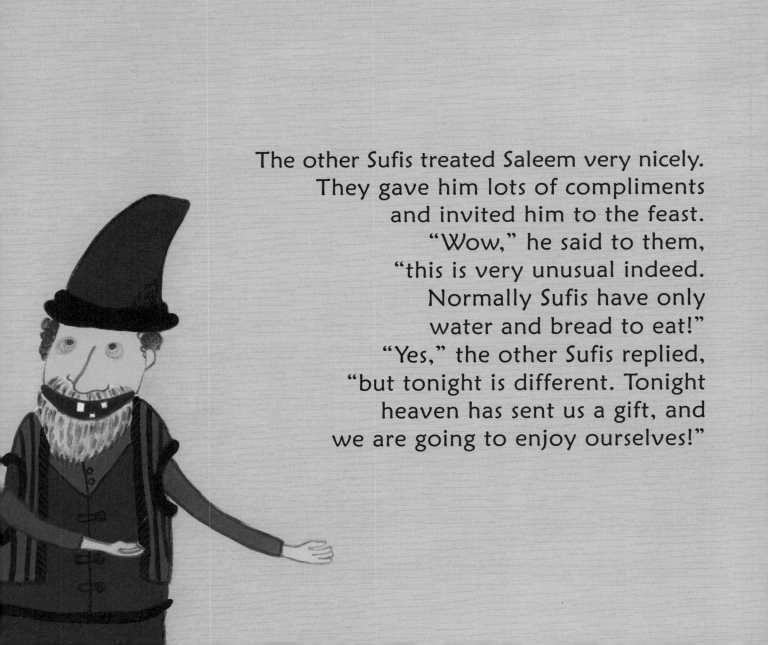

The other Sufis treated Saleem very nicely.
They gave him lots of compliments
and invited him to the feast.
"Wow," he said to them,
"this is very unusual indeed.
Normally Sufis have only
water and bread to eat!"
"Yes," the other Sufis replied,
"but tonight is different. Tonight
heaven has sent us a gift, and
we are going to enjoy ourselves!"

So Saleem joined the other Sufis,
eating and drinking like
he hadn't done in a long time.
After dinner, the musicians
started to play, and the Sufis
began to dance and whirl.

Saleem joined in the dance,
sometimes bowing his head to the ground . . .

. . . sometimes raising his arms to the sky.

Then suddenly the musicians picked up the beat,
and one of them started to sing a song.
"The donkey's gone,
the donkey's gone,"
he sang, over
and over.

One by one the Sufis joined in the singing.
Saleem did not know this song,
but he didn't want to be left out,
so he started to imitate
the other Sufis, singing along:
"The donkey's gone,
the donkey's gone . . ."

So they sang and
so they danced,
late into the night,
until they all passed out
from exhaustion.

In the morning Saleem woke to see
that all the other Sufis had already
gone their separate ways.
He shook the dust from his clothes,
then went to get his donkey
and continue his journey.
But when he got to the stable,
it was empty.

Saleem ran to the stable boy.
"Where's my donkey?" he said.
"What have you done with him?"

The stable boy replied: "Don't you know?
The other Sufis took your donkey
to town last night, and sold it!
That's how they paid for all the food
and the musicians!"

Saleem became very angry. "I trusted you with my donkey!" he yelled. "It's all I had in this world! Couldn't you at least come and tell me before the other Sufis had left? Maybe I could have made them pay me for my donkey— or get me another one!"

"I tried," said the stable boy.
"I came inside a few times
to tell you; but each time, I saw that you were
dancing with the other Sufis, and singing,
'The donkey's gone, the donkey's gone!'
So I figured you knew very well what was going on,
and you didn't mind!"

"It's my own fault," Saleem realized. "That's what can happen when you mindlessly imitate other people—sometimes you end up losing what's most precious to you!"

So he went on his way,
having lost his donkey
but learned his lesson.

Iranian-American scholar and teacher OMID ARABIAN is the founder and director of YOUniversal Center, where he conducts courses in mysticism for adults and children. His translations of Rumi's poetry have been published in three volumes. He lives and works in Los Angeles.

SHILLA SHAKOORI is a contemporary artist from Tehran, Iran, currently based in Los Angeles. In her art, Shilla seeks to bring together her native and adopted cultures. She credits Rumi with helping her connect to her cultural heritage and go beyond it.

RUMI is the great Persian mystic who lived eight centuries ago but remains among the world's most beloved poets today. His poems and stories, carrying messages of universal love and self-empowerment, have inspired truth seekers throughout the ages.

A TRIANGLE SQUARE BOOK FOR YOUNG READERS
PUBLISHED BY SEVEN STORIES PRESS

SEVEN STORIES PRESS
140 Watts Street
New York, NY 10013
www.sevenstories.com

College professors and high school and middle school teachers may order free examination copies of Seven Stories Press titles. Visit https://www.sevenstories.com/pg/resources-academics or email academics@sevenstories.com.

Library of Congress Cataloging-in-Publication Data

Names: Arabian, Omid, author. | Shakoori, Shilla, illustrator. | Jalāl al-Dīn Rūmī, Maulana, 1207-1273.
Title: The donkey's gone! : based on a story by Rumi / text, Omid Arabian ; illustrations, Shilla Shakoori.
Description: New York, N.Y. : Seven Stories Press, [2021] Based on a story from The Masnavi by the 13th century Sufi mystic Rumi.
Audience: Ages 4-9. | Audience: Grades K-1. | Summary: Saleem the Sufi, who travels the world on his much-loved donkey, stops at a Sufi monastery where that night the monks are celebrating with a lavish dinner, music, and dancing because they have been given a gift from heaven; Saleem joins in the festivities, only to discover in the morning that the "gift" was his donkey which was sold to pay for the celebration, and he leaves the monastery, on foot, a sad but wiser man.
Identifiers: LCCN 2021022763 (print) | LCCN 2021022764 (ebook) | ISBN 9781644210901 (hardcover) | ISBN 9781644210918 (ebook)
Subjects: LCSH: Sufis--Juvenile fiction. | Donkeys--Juvenile fiction. | Sufi parables--Juvenile fiction. | Conduct of life--Juvenile fiction. | Humorous stories.
CYAC: Sufis--Fiction. | Donkeys--Fiction. | Conduct of life--Fiction. | Humorous stories. | LCGFT: Parables. | Humorous fiction.
Classification: LCC PZ7.1.A69 Do 2021 (print) | LCC PZ7.1.A69 (ebook)
DDC [E]--dc23
LC record available at https://lccn.loc.gov/2021022763
LC ebook record available at https://lccn.loc.gov/2021022764

Printed in China.

9 8 7 6 5 4 3 2 1